THE ADVENTURES OF TOM SAWYER

by MARK TWAIN

# #2 The Best Fence Painter

Adapted by Catherine Nichols

Illustrated by Amy Bates

**Sterling Publishing Co., Inc.**
New York

**visit us at www.abdopublishing.com**

Reinforced library bound edition published in 2008 by Spotlight, a division of the ABDO Publishing Group, 8000 West 78th Street, Edina, Minnesota 55439. Published by agreement with Sterling Publishing Co., Inc.

Originally published and © 2004 by Barnes and Noble, Inc.
Illustrations © 2004 by Amy Bates
Cover Illustration by Amy Bates

**Library of Congress Cataloging-in-Publication Data**
This title was previously cataloged with the following information:
Nichols, Catherine.
    The adventures of Tom Sawyer. #2, The best fence painter / by Mark Twain ; adapted by Catherine Nichols ; illustrated by Amy Bates.
        p. cm. -- (Easy reader classics)
    Summary: A brief, simplified retelling of the episode in "Tom Sawyer" in which Tom whitewashes a fence.
    [1. Behavior--Fiction. 2. Missouri--Fiction.] I. Bates, Amy, ill. II. Twain, Mark, 1835-1910. III. Title: Adventures of Tom Sawyer. IV. Title.
PZ7.N5288 Adw 2006
[E]--dc22                                                        2005026323
ISBN 978-1-59961-335-2 (reinforced library bound edition)

# Contents

## Too Much Work

It was Saturday.
The sun was shining.
What a wonderful day
Tom Sawyer had planned!
He was going fishing
down by the river.
He got his fishing pole.
"Not so fast!" said Aunt Polly.

Tom's aunt had a bucket of paint.

She also had some brushes.

"Are you painting?" asked Tom.

"No, Tom," Aunt Polly said.
"*You* are going to paint.
You are going to paint
the fence outside.
*Then* you may go fishing."

Tom walked over to the fence.

How very long it was!

It seemed to go on and on.

He felt tired just looking at it.

Tom dipped a brush
into the white paint.
He painted for a bit.
His work looked good!

Then Tom looked at all
he still had to do.
"I will never finish!" he said.
How he wished he didn't
have to paint the fence!
How he wished to go fishing!

Then Tom saw his friend
Ben Rogers down the street.
Suddenly, Tom had an idea.
He knew a way to paint the fence
without doing any of the work!

## Tom's Plan

Tom started painting again.
As he worked, he hummed.
Ben walked up to Tom.
"Hello, Tom," Ben said.
"Too bad you have to work,
and on a Saturday, too."
Ben did *not* sound sorry.

Ben took a bite of his apple.

Tom's mouth watered.

How he wanted that apple!

"I'm going fishing," Ben said.

"I guess you can't come.

Not with all that work to do!"

"Work?" Tom said. "*Work?*"
"*This* isn't work to me!
I can fish any old time,
but I don't get to paint
every day, do I?"

Ben watched Tom paint.

It did look like fun.

"*I* want to paint!" Ben said.

"I don't know . . ." said Tom.

"You can have an apple," Ben said.

"Well, okay," said Tom.

Tom sat under a tree.
He ate the tasty apple.
He watched as Ben
did his chore for him.
His plan was working!

## The Sweet Life

After Tom finished the apple,
his friend Billy Fisher came by.
Billy saw Ben painting,
and Billy's jaw dropped.
"That is *Tom's* fence!" Billy said.
"Why are *you* painting it, Ben?"

"I want to," Ben said,
"and Tom is letting me
because *I'm* his friend."

Billy went over to Tom.

"*I* want to paint, too," said Billy.

"I don't know . . ." Tom said.

"You can have my lollipop," said Billy.

He gave it to Tom.

Tom gave Billy a brush.

Then more of Tom's
friends passed by.
Each one wanted
to paint the fence.
Tom let all the boys
have a turn . . . as long as
they gave him a treat.

Soon Tom was stuffed with goodies
*and* he had painted the fence
without doing any of the work.
He was the best fence painter ever!

## All Done!

Tom could not wait
to tell Aunt Polly
he was done painting.
Now she would
let him go fishing!
Tom ran inside.

"May I go fishing?" Tom asked.

"So soon?" asked his aunt.

"How much of the fence
did you paint?"

"All of it," Tom said.

"*All* of it?" asked Aunt Polly.

"So soon, Tom Sawyer?
How could that be?"

"Come see!" Tom said.

Aunt Polly and Tom went outside.

"You did finish!" she said.

"I'm so pleased, Tom.

Come, I have a reward

for you, my dear."

Aunt Polly took out donuts.

"I baked these today," she said.

Tom took a big bite of one.

His tummy started to hurt.

He remembered all the sweets
he had already eaten.
He moaned and groaned.
"My tummy hurts!" he said.
So Aunt Polly quickly
sent him off to bed.

Tom saw his friends
outside his window.
They had fishing poles.
"We're going fishing," Ben said.
"Do you want to come?"

Tom sure did,
but Aunt Polly said,
"Sorry, boys.
Tom's tummy hurts.
He can't go fishing."

Then she gave Tom medicine.
*Ugh!* It tasted *awful.*

How Tom wished he had not
eaten so very many treats!
He promised himself next time
he *would* be the best fence painter—
one who didn't fool his friends—
one who painted his fence himself!